THE PRINCE WHO KNEW HIS FATE

An ancient Egyptian tale
translated from hieroglyphs
and illustrated by
Lise Manniche

The Metropolitan Museum of Art/Philomel Books New York

There once was a king of Egypt who had no sons at all. So the king asked the gods of his time for a son and they decided that he should have one.

That night the king slept with his wife. She became pregnant, and when the months of child-bearing had passed she bore him a son.

The seven Hathor goddesses came to decide the boy's fate and they declared, "He is destined to be killed by a crocodile or a snake or a dog."

The people who were at the boy's side heard this. They reported it to the king and his heart grew sad.

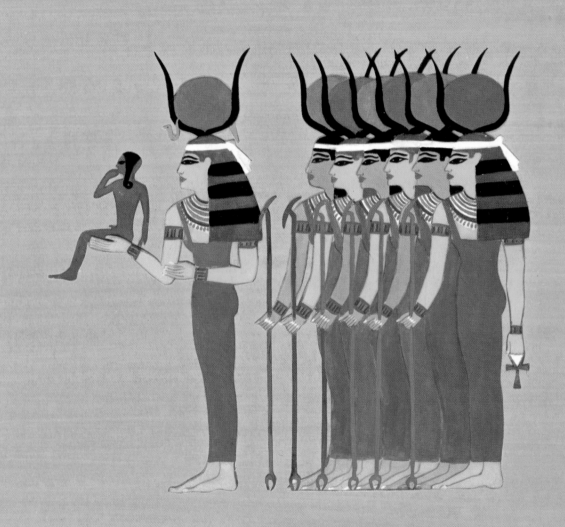

The king had a house of stone built for the boy at the edge of the desert, supplied with servants and with all sorts of good things from the palace, for the child was not to go outside. There the boy grew up.

One day he climbed up to the roof of the house and saw a dog following a man, who was walking along the road.

"What is that?" he asked his servant.

"It's a dog," the servant replied.

"Let me have a dog like that," the boy said.

The servant reported this to the king and the king said, "His heart is sad.
Let him have a bounding little puppy."

So they gave the boy a dog.

In time, the young prince grew restless and he sent a message to his father, saying, "Why should I stay here doing nothing? After all, my destiny has been determined. Allow me to do as I wish until I meet my fate."

The king replied saying "Let a chariot be prepared for him, equipped with all sorts of weapons, and assign a servant to accompany him."

So they did as the king commanded and gave him all that he needed. Then they ferried him across the Nile to the east bank and said to him, "Now go as you wish."

And the dog was with him.

The prince traveled as he pleased
northwards across the desert,
living on the best of all the
desert game.

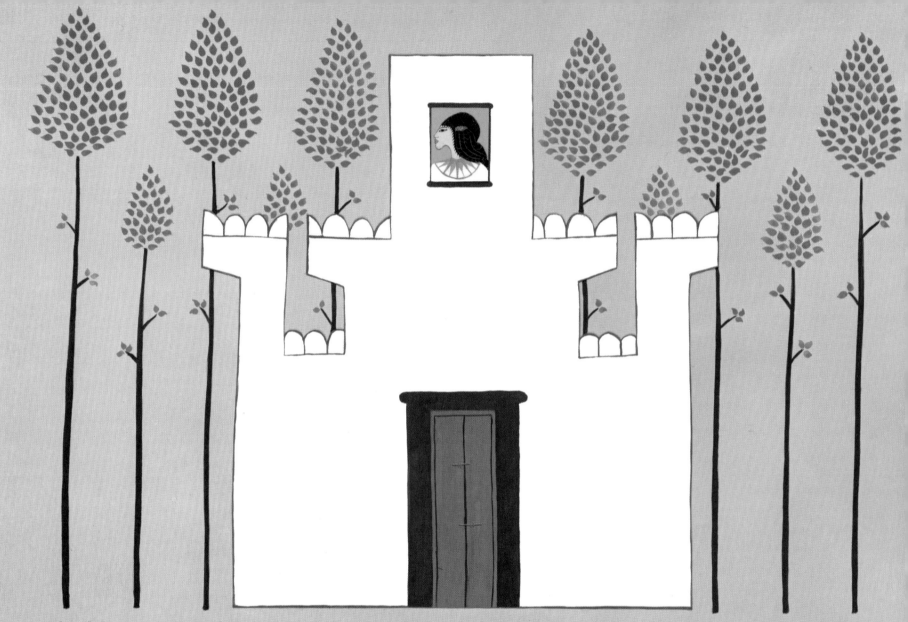

Thus he came to the realm of the Chief of Naharín, who had no children — except one daughter. He had built a house for her with a window seventy cubits from the ground.

The Chief of Naharín then sent for all the sons of all the chiefs of Kharu, saying, "He who can jump up to the window of my daughter shall have her for his wife."

The sons of all the chiefs had been trying to reach the window each day for many days when the prince passed by them.

They took the prince to their house, and they bathed him, they rubbed him with oil, and they bandaged his feet. They gave fodder to his horses and food to his servant. They did everything for the young man.

And to start a conversation, they said, "Where do you come from, you handsome youth?"

"I am the son of a chariot officer from Egypt. My mother died and my father took another wife. My stepmother grew to hate me and I have fled from her."

They welcomed him and kissed him.

Several days later the prince asked the youths, "What are you doing here in Naharín?"

"The past three months we have spent each day jumping, for the Chief of Naharín will give his daughter to the one who reaches her window," they said.

"Oh, if only I could enchant my feet, I would jump with you," said the prince.

The youths went off to jump, as it was their daily custom, while the prince stood at a distance, watching.

From her window the daughter of the Chief of Naharín gazed at him.

At last, when many days had passed, the prince joined the sons of the chiefs.

He jumped and he reached the window of the daughter of the Chief of Naharín.

She embraced him and she kissed him.

A messenger went to inform her father.

"One of the young men has reached the window of your daughter," the messenger said.

"Whose son is it?" the Chief of Naharín inquired.

"He is the son of a chariot officer from Egypt. He has fled from his stepmother."

The Chief of Naharìn grew very angry. "Am I to give my daughter to a fugitive from Egypt? Send him home!"

"You must go back where you came from," the messenger said to the prince.

But the princess clung to the prince, and she swore, "As Re lives, if they take him from me, I will not eat, I will not drink, I will die within the hour!"

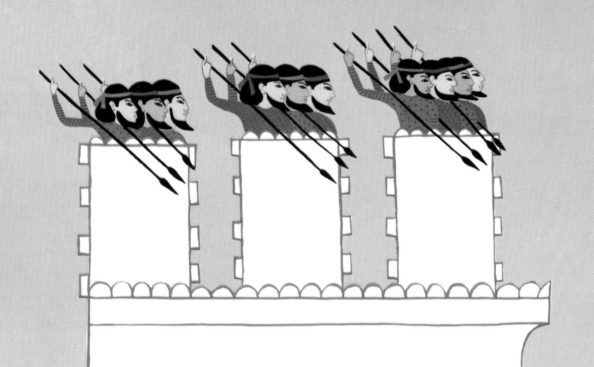

When the messenger had reported everything she had said to her father, her father sent men to kill the prince then and there.

Again the princess swore, "As Re lives, if they kill him, I shall die before sunset. I will not live an hour more than he!"

They repeated this to her father, and the Chief of Naharín had the prince and his daughter brought before him.

The young man impressed the Chief, who welcomed him and kissed him and said, "Now you are like my own son. Tell me about yourself."

"I am the child of a chariot officer from Egypt," said the young man. "My mother died and my father took another wife. She grew to hate me, and I have fled from her."

𓈖𓏭𓅠𓏏𓆑𓏤𓏏𓊪𓅠𓃀𓉔𓆓𓈖𓈖𓀠𓏏𓊪𓊪𓅠𓏭𓈖𓀠𓅠𓏏𓊪𓅠𓈖𓈖𓇋𓉔

The Chief of Naharín gave his daughter to the prince,
and he gave him a house and fields and herds and
everything they needed.

When they had lived together for some time, the young man told his wife, "I know my fate. I shall be killed by one of three: a crocodile or a snake or a dog."

"Then," she said, "the dog that follows you everywhere must be killed."

"That would be folly," he replied. "I will not have the dog killed for I have had it ever since it was a puppy."

So his wife began to watch over him closely, and she did not allow him to go out alone.

It so happened that on the very day the prince had arrived in Naharín, the crocodile, his fate, began to follow him. It caught up with him in the town where the prince lived with his wife.

But there in the lake was a giant who would not let the crocodile out, and so the crocodile refused to let the giant out. For three whole months they had been fighting all day long, beginning each day at sunrise.

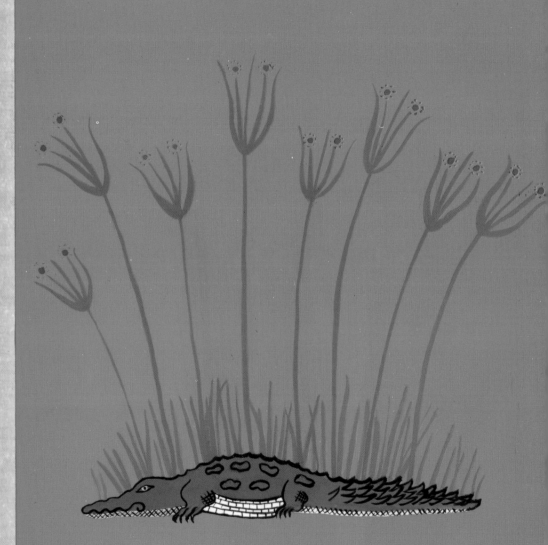

The prince spent many pleasant days in his house, and in the evenings when the breeze died down, he went to bed. One evening when sleep had overcome him, his wife filled a vessel with wine and another with beer. Then she sat down beside him, but she did not sleep.

A snake came out of its hole intending to bite the prince, but the vessels tempted it and the snake drank from them, got drunk and rolled over on its back to sleep.

His wife chopped the snake in three pieces with her axe. Then she roused her husband and said to him, "See, your god has placed one of your fates in your hands. He is protecting you."

The prince made offerings to his god Re, adoring him and exalting his power each day that passed.

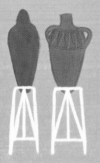

After some time, the prince went for a stroll around his estate. His wife stayed at home, but his dog followed him.

Suddenly the dog turned on him and the prince fled from it.

He ran to the edge of the lake and jumped into the water to escape the dog, but there the crocodile seized him and dragged him off to find the giant.

"I am pursuing you, for I am your fate," said the crocodile. "Listen, for three whole months I have been fighting with the giant. I will let you go now if you will take my side and kill the giant when he returns to fight."

So the prince waited by the water all that night, and when dawn broke and a second day began, the giant returned.

The giant began to fight the crocodile at once, but the prince stepped forward with his scimitar in his hand. He cut out the heart of the giant and the giant died.

At that very moment the dog sneaked up behind the prince. It attacked him and tore him to bits and spread the pieces all about.

When the prince failed to return, his wife set out to look for him. After seven days and seven nights in search of him, she came upon his remains.

She collected all the pieces of her husband's body and put them back together again — except for his heart. That she placed in a lotus flower which was blooming on the water.

Lo and behold, the prince reappeared as he had been before.

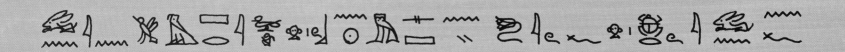

From that day on the prince and princess lived together happily until they crossed over to the fields of the blessed.

With the help of the writer, Lise Manniche, the story has reached a happy end. Those who speak evil of it will have to contend with Thoth, the god of the scribes.

About the story and the illustrations

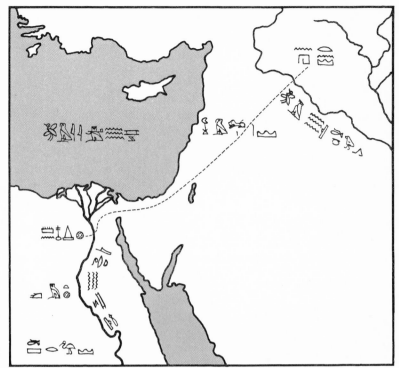

The *Prince Who Knew His Fate* is one of the oldest fairy tales known today. It was written down by an Egyptian scribe more than 3000 years ago and I have translated the tale from the hieroglyphs for this book. The original papyrus manuscript is now in the British Museum in London.

The prince and princess in the tale may once really have lived, for the ancient Egyptians often made up tales with real kings and important persons as the main characters. We can only surmise who the prince and princess were, however, for their names are never mentioned in the papyrus. Perhaps they were relatives of the famous Queen Nefertiti and the young King Tutankhamun. Many details lead us to believe that the story was written down during their lifetime.

The places in the story were real places. Naharin was a princedom east of the river Euphrates in what is now called Iraq; and Kharu, the home of the other princes, was in Syria. We know that several princesses from Naharin did come to the court of the Egyptian king about the time this story was written.

In those days one of the royal palaces was in Memphis, near modern Cairo, and this may be where the prince lived in his desert house. When he left home, he crossed the Nile and traveled over the eastern desert until he came to the land of Naharin, where he won the princess. Here I have drawn a map, marking his route, and you can read the ancient names in hieroglyphs.

Kemet   The black land ⎫
Desheret   The red land ⎭ (Egypt)

Iteru aa   The great river (The Nile)

Men nefer   The good resting place (Memphis)

Naharin   A princedom in Iraq

Pa mu kedu   The opposite water (The Euphrates)

Kharu   A princedom in Syria

Pa im   The sea (The Mediterranean)

There are no pictures in the original papyrus scroll. To illustrate this book I have copied Egyptian artwork done during the time the story probably took place.

The ship and the cattle, for example, are copied from a wall painting in a tomb; the chariot in the desert from a painted box that once belonged to King Tutankhamun; and the house built in the desert from a drawing on a papyrus scroll.

Most of the other illustrations are copied from reliefs carved on slabs of stone. This relief, on a sandstone block from Thebes, Egypt, that is now in the Cleveland Museum of Art, served as the model for the prince:

It may be a picture of Nefertiti or her husband, King Akhenaten. We cannot tell which for they both wore the same kind of wig; the decoration, which would give us a clue, is missing. If the wig is decorated with one cobra, it is the king; if it has two cobras, it is the queen.

The model for the princess is this lady at the royal court pictured in a relief on a limestone block from el-Amarna in the Norbert Schimmel Collection, on loan at The Metropolitan Museum of Art in New York:

These reliefs were once painted in bright colors that have since disappeared. It was not difficult, however, to figure out how they were painted originally. The ancient Egyptians always used the same color for the same subject, once they had decided what color it should be. And they rarely mixed their colors in varying tints or shades.

The skin of Egyptian men was always colored a brownish-red. Women and people from Asia were always shown with yellow skin. Green was used for all that grows, and blue was the color of the sky and water. Black was used to represent what was black in nature; but it was also used to symbolize fertility and rebirth, like the black mud left on the banks of the Nile after a flood. White was for garments, bread, and other things that are held sacred.

Drawing on papyrus in The Brooklyn Museum

In the original papyrus, the giant killed by the prince is called *nekhet,* which means "strong." In another papyrus, I found this creature (at left) who is also called *nekhet.* So I decided to make him the giant in the story of the prince.

The *nekhet* has a big head and a plump body; he has the tail of a crocodile, the back of a bird, and large outstretched wings. His feet are jackals' heads, and piled up on his wig is a collection of frightening animals—lions, a falcon, a snake, and a jackal. At the very top of the headdress is a figure that indicates the giant will live for a million years: the man holding his arms up stands for "one million" and the palm branch signifies "year," all of which really means "forever."

I think the prince had to use magic as well as his scimitar to kill such a terrifying opponent.

The Chief of Naharin is a grim man with yellow skin and a big beard. I found this Asian on the side of a chariot that once belonged to an Egyptian king. He is pictured kneeling, his arms tied with a rope, for the Egyptian king has taken him prisoner. To restore him to dignity as the Chief of Naharin, I had to take his limbs apart and rearrange him on a throne.

The models for the other Asiatic princes are carved on a slab of stone from an Egyptian tomb, now kept in Leiden, Holland. Here I found them standing as if they had assembled to greet the prince upon his arrival in Naharin. The problem then was how to draw these princes moving and jumping as they tried to reach the window of the princess.

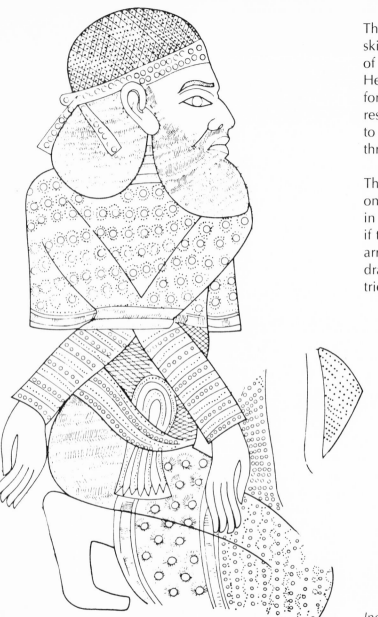

Incised figure on the chariot of Tutankhamun, in the Egyptian Museum, Cairo

This relief is found in the temple of Medinet Habu in Thebes. It shows an Egyptian king in his chariot, raging against his enemies, the Libyans. The poor foreigners are cast helter-skelter under the royal horses. I rescued some of them, placed them upright, dressed them in the garments of the princes—and there they are in this book, jumping as high as they can. Perhaps you can find the models among the fallen Libyans in this drawing of the relief.

Before the story was written down, the Egyptians had had many gods. That is why the king turned to the "gods of his time" when he wanted a son.

Then, about the time the story was recorded, something quite extraordinary had happened: King Akhenaten had decreed that only one of the gods, Re-Harakhte the sun god, was to be worshipped in Egypt. Re-Harakhte had the head of a falcon, symbolizing the sun that traveled across the sky like a falcon.

Not only did King Akhenaten dispose of all the other gods, but he also changed the appearance of Re-Harakhte because the falcon head reminded him of the old gods. He decided that Re-Harakhte should be depicted as a sun disc with its rays ending in little hands. This was the prince's god.

In Naharin there were no temples for Re-Harakhte where the prince could make his offerings. So he may have used a small altar in his own house like the one in this relief, which shows Akhenaten offering (from the top) 3 bowls of burning incense, 2 bunches of grapes, 1 cucumber, 1 bunch of flowers, 3 round loaves of bread, 3 chunks of meat, 4 ducks, 3 ribs of meat, 3 joints of beef, and 3 heads of oxen lying on some greenery. Akhenaten is holding 2 vases: they probably contain water. Akhenaten's head is missing—was actually removed—from the relief but I have given him one in my drawing.

The Egyptians made offerings because they believed that the gods—even the sun disc—needed food and drink like human beings. (By the end of the day, all these delicacies were eaten by the priests in the temples.)

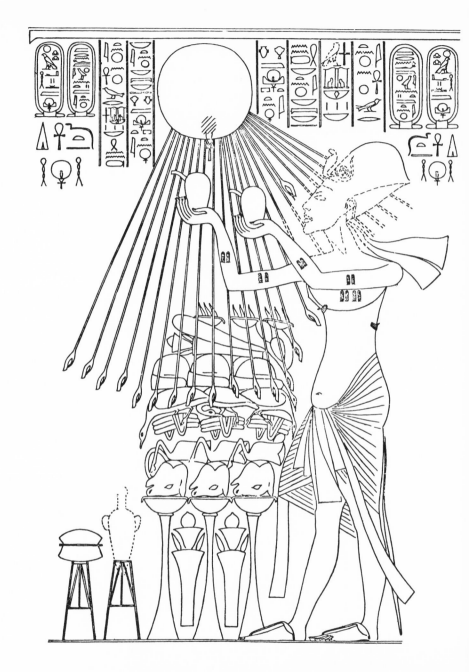

Relief in the tomb of Tutu, el-Amarna

When the prince was born, the seven Hathor goddesses, like the fairy godmothers in other more modern tales, came to decide his fate. He would be killed by a snake, a dog, or a crocodile, they decreed. These three animals were both loved and hated by the ancient Egyptians.

The Egyptians were afraid of snakes. So in order to make friends with them, they treated them as gods and tried not to harm them. If by accident they were bitten by a snake, they went to see the doctor, who had magic formulas for driving the poison out of a person's body. The formulas did not always help!

There were many different kinds of snakes in Egypt. Some of them lived in the Netherworld, where they tried to kill the sun. One of these monsters was the model for the snake, who became the Prince's first fate.

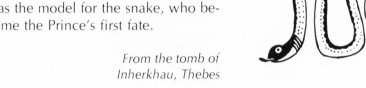

*From the tomb of
Inherkhau, Thebes*

The model for the prince's dog is a kind of Greyhound, or saluki, one of the favorite Egyptian breeds.

The ancient Egyptians had pet dogs, as we do today, and they gave them names like "Blackie," "Good Guardian," and "Faithful." Dogs were used for hunting, and they accompanied soldiers at war.

Many dogs were stray animals, however, running about in the streets or in the desert, packs of them pestering people for food and keeping everybody awake at night.

*From an unguent jar of
Tutankhamun in the
Egyptian Museum, Cairo*

The crocodile was a daily threat and a fearful fate to meet. It lurked in the canals, waiting to snatch the newborn calves when the shepherd drove his cattle across the water. At each crossing the shepherd would shout a magic formula, hoping to ward them off. Women were afraid of encountering crocodiles when they went to fetch water from the river, and the shipwrecked sailors or travelers always swam swiftly toward shore to avoid them.

There was a crocodile god, who had a temple all to himself where the sacred crocodiles lived. They wore golden bracelets and earrings and were served their favorite foods each day. When they died, the priests in the temple had them made into mummies.

From the papyrus of Here-ubekhet in the Egyptian Museum, Cairo

One of these three animals would take the life of the prince, but the prince could not know which one it would be.

In fact, no one knows how the original story of *The Prince Who Knew His Fate* ended, for the papyrus scroll is torn just where the crocodile seizes the prince and says, "... if you will kill the giant ...." So I had to invent an ending to the tale myself, as I think the ancient scribe may have written it.

The prince had to meet his fate, for in ancient Egypt a man could not escape his destiny. The prince had already been saved from the snake, and he was about to make a bargain with the crocodile. So, only the dog was left, the dog who had followed him—perhaps ominously—from the very beginning. The dog must have taken the prince's life. Yet the tales of that time usually had happy endings. Somehow I had to bring the prince back to life again.

In the Egyptian legend of Osiris, the King of the Dead, I found half of the solution. When Osiris is killed and his body torn apart, his wife, Isis, collects the pieces and puts them together again. So I let the princess follow Isis' example; but still the prince could not move about or speak.

The rest of the solution I found in an ancient belief. The Egyptians liked to imagine that, after death, they would be reborn, just as the sun was born when the world was created, bursting forth from a lotus blossom. To bring about his own rebirth—for example—a man named Ani had buried in his tomb a scroll of papyrus with a drawing of himself coming out of the lotus flower.

So I think the prince was finally saved because the princess placed his heart in a lotus flower.

The prince and princess did not live happily only "to the end of their days" as some modern fairy tales would have it. They believed that, at the end of their days in this life, they would sail across the river Nile to a new life in the Fields of the Blessed.

To conclude the story in ancient style, I have invoked the protection of the god of the scribes, Thoth.

Lise Manniche

From the papyrus of Ani,
British Museum, London

Library of Congress Cataloging in Publication Data
Main entry under title:

The Prince who knew his fate.

Summary: Retells the 3,000 year-old Egyptian tale of the prince whose fate, to die by a crocodile, a snake, or a dog, is decreed at his birth. Includes additional information about the background of the story and the civilization of ancient Egypt.
[1. Fairy tales.   2. Folklore—Egypt.   3. Egypt—Civilization]
I. Manniche, Lise, ill.
PZ8.P9386   398.2'1'0962   81-10740
ISBN 0-87099-278-3 (MMA)   AACR2
ISBN 0-399-20850-X (Philomel)

I am greatly indebted to J. R. Harris and P. J. Frandsen for suggestions in translating and completing the tale.

L. M.

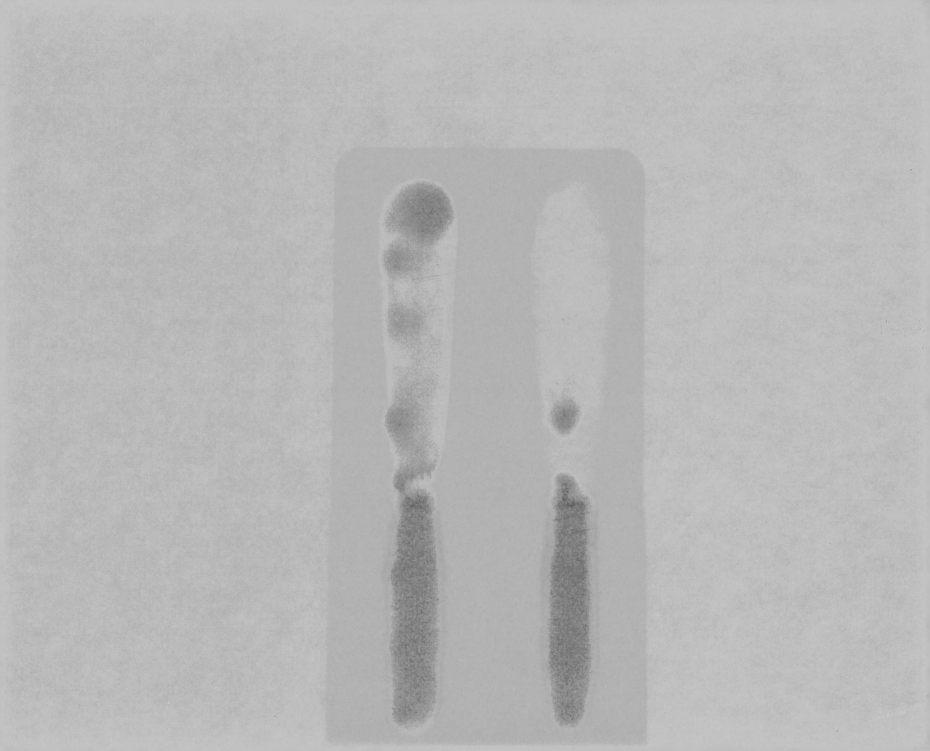